Teeny Tiny

Teeny Tiny

Pictures by Tomie de Paola
Story retold by Jill Bennett

Oxford University Press
Oxford Toronto Melbourne

For Colin

Oxford University Press, Walton Street, Oxford OX2 6DP

Oxford New York Toronto
Delhi Bombay Calcutta Madras Karachi
Petaling Jaya Singapore Hong Kong Tokyo
Nairobi Dar es Salaam Cape Town
Melbourne Auckland

and associated companies in
Berlin Ibadan

Oxford is a trade mark of Oxford University Press

First Published 1985
Reprinted 1987
First published in paperback 1988

British Library Cataloguing in Publication Data

Bennett, Jill, *1947–*
  Teeny tiny.
  I. Title   II. De Paola, Tomie
  823'.914[F]   PZ7

ISBN 0–19–278205–3 (Hardbook)
ISBN 0–19–272194–1 (Paperback)

Typeset by Oxford Publishing Services
Printed in Hong Kong

Once upon a time there was a
teeny tiny woman who lived
in a teeny tiny house
in a teeny tiny village.

One day this teeny tiny woman
put on her teeny tiny hat

and went out of her
teeny tiny house
to take a teeny tiny walk.

When the teeny tiny woman
had gone a teeny tiny way
she came to a teeny tiny gate.

So the teeny tiny woman
opened the teeny tiny gate
and went into a
teeny tiny churchyard.

In the teeny tiny churchyard
she saw a teeny tiny bone
on a teeny tiny grave

and the teeny tiny woman
said to her teeny tiny self,
'This teeny tiny bone
will make some
teeny tiny soup
for my teeny tiny supper.'

And so the teeny tiny woman
took the teeny tiny bone
from the teeny tiny grave
and put it in her
teeny tiny pocket

and went back to
her teeny tiny house.

When the teeny tiny woman
got to her teeny tiny house
she was a teeny tiny bit tired.

So she went up her teeny tiny stairs

and put the teeny tiny bone
into her teeny tiny cupboard

and got into her
teeny tiny bed.

When the teeny tiny woman
had been asleep for
a teeny tiny while
she was awakened
by a teeny tiny voice
from the teeny tiny cupboard
which said,

'GIVE ME MY BONE!'

And the teeny tiny woman
was a teeny tiny bit frightened,

so she hid her teeny tiny head
under the teeny tiny bedclothes
and went to sleep again.

And when she had slept
a teeny tiny time
the teeny tiny voice
cried out again
from the teeny tiny cupboard
a teeny tiny bit louder,

'GIVE ME MY BONE!'

This made the teeny tiny woman
a teeny tiny bit more frightened,

so she hid her teeny tiny head
a teeny tiny bit further
under the teeny tiny bedclothes.

And when the teeny tiny woman
had been asleep again
for a teeny tiny time,
the teeny tiny voice
from the teeny tiny cupboard
said a teeny tiny bit louder,

'GIVE ME MY BONE!'

The teeny tiny woman
was a teeny tiny bit
more frightened,

but she popped her teeny tiny head
out of the teeny tiny bedclothes
and said in her loudest
teeny tiny voice,